THE PERILS OF
CHESTER

DAISY VENTRESS

Illustrated by Amanda L. Matthews

Outskirts Press, Inc.
http://www.outskirtspress.com

ISBN: 978-1-9772-3963-1

Cover & interior illustrations by Amanda L. Matthews

Outskirts Press and the "OP" logo are trademarks belonging to Outskirts Press, Inc.

PRINTED IN THE UNITED STATES OF AMERICA

This Book Belongs to:

Once upon a time, there were two miniature turtles that were looking for a new family.

The turtles were brother and sister and their mom were swept away into the ocean. The two tiny turtles were left ashore all alone.

A small boy named Kevin, who was 5 years old, was playing with a ball on the beach. Suddenly, he spotted two turtles stuck in a sand trap unable to swim back into the ocean. Kevin rescued the turtles from the sand and put them in his pocket. Kevin was having a picnic with his mother and brother on Venice Beach to celebrate the 4th of July. Kevin was bursting with excitement and he really wanted to ask his mom if he could take the turtles home.

Kevin hid his new little friends from his family. When his mom was not watching, Kevin carefully took the turtles out of his pocket and fed them small pieces of strawberries and carrots from the picnic basket. Kevin really wanted to keep the turtles as pets. And he knew that his dad would have said yes if he was still alive. Kevin's dad died just a few months earlier. Kevin really missed his dad, and his mom and brother were also always very sad. Kevin did not want to ask his mom right now because he knew that she cried every night after Kevin and his brother went to bed. So, Kevin quietly put the 2 turtles in his pocket for the long ride home. Kevin decided to tell his mom and brother about his new friends the next day. He hoped that his new pets would soften his family's pain and bring joy back into their home.

After playing with the turtles for a few hours, Kevin gave them both names. He named his new little friends Chester and Julie. Kevin filled his old Goldfish bowl with water and put Chester and Julie inside the bowl. He then placed them safely under his bed. After that, Kevin, Chester, and Julie had a good night's sleep.

Kevin's mom frowned when she learned that he brought the turtles home without asking her permission. But she decided that the turtles could stay because she knew how much Kevin missed his Dad and she saw that the turtles brought Kevin great happiness.

Kevin loved Chester and Julie and he watched them play in the Goldfish bowl for hours. Kevin fed the turtles every day after he finished his other chores. Chester and Julie had small pieces of apple for dinner and were lying around lazily on the rocks when Kevin gently lifted them out of the tank for some exercise. Chester and Julie took slow walks on Kevin's homework desk. Chester and Julie would race toward the end of the desk, it was always a tie. Kevin smiled at the turtles and thought about how proud his dad would be if he could see how well he took care of his turtles.

Summer ended and it was almost time for Kevin to return to school as a first grader. Kevin woke up early and decided to give Chester and Julie a ride on his head for fun! Kevin placed the turtles in his hair on the very top of his head and started to run around his room. Chester had a larger shell and went flying to the floor! Kevin feared Chester was hurt and carefully put him back into the Goldfish bowl. Chester started to swim quickly over the rocks and took a bite of some fruit that was left over from dinner. Chester raised his head high and stretched out his little neck and then fell fast asleep. Julie joined Chester and swam around the tank for a while and soon also fell asleep.

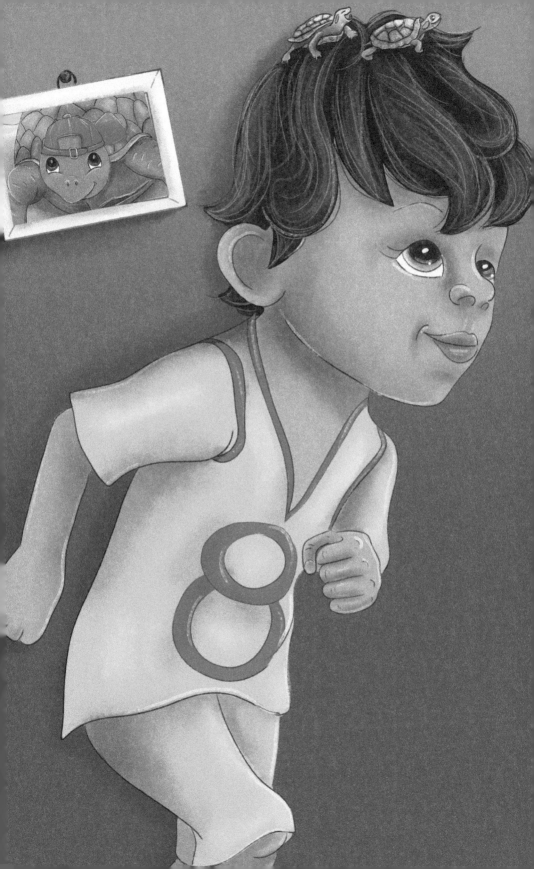

Kevin attended his first day of school and he shared with his new class that he adopted two turtles over the summer. His classmates were curious about the turtles because most of them had cats or dogs. Kevin asked the teacher if he could bring the turtles to school to show his classmates. The teacher said no because it was against school rules. Kevin did not want to disappoint his friends and he wanted to show off Chester and Julie. Their bodies were green, and their shells were about the size of a quarter. Kevin had a great idea! He did not want to disobey the teacher but wanted to show his friends the turtles. So, after school Kevin asked a few friends to meet him at the playground. He rode his bike home as fast as he could, ran inside the house, grabbed the turtles from the tank and placed Chester and Julie in his pocket. Kevin ran all the way back to the playground in the school yard to meet friends carrying Chester and Julie is his pockets.

Once Kevin arrived at the playground, he saw the 10 children waiting to see his turtles. He felt happy and thrilled to show off his new pets. Kevin reached into his pockets but there were no turtles there. His pockets were totally empty! He lost the turtles somewhere along the path from his house to the playground. Kevin knew he had to act quickly because Chester and Julie were in danger of being eaten by the neighborhood cat, Sam. Sam was always hungry and on the prowl for food.

Kevin and his friends searched the entire path back to his house but did not find the turtles. Kevin was very sad and feared that the turtles were lost forever. Kevin went home, sat on his bed, and cried. He remembered feeling the same sadness when his dad went to heaven. A few minutes later, there was a knock on his door and Kevin's mother saw him crying and learned that the turtles were lost. Kevin's mother explained to him that sometimes-bad things happen when children do not obey the rules. Kevin's mom decided the family should go out and look for the turtles one more time before dark.

Kevin's family was on their hands and knees searching his room, the grass, bushes, and the road and bike path for hours hoping to find Chester and Julie. The family noticed the hungry cat Sam lurking around the playground. Kevin was worried that the turtles may have been Sam's dinner. They made their way back to the house and to everyone's surprise Chester and Julie were walking slowly on the sidewalk toward home! The Family shouted, "Hooray"! Kevin scooped Chester and Julie up, gave them a gently pat on their heads, and took them to their Goldfish bowl where they were finally safe and sound.

Kevin asked his mother for permission to invite a few friends over the long Labor Day weekend to watch Chester and Julie swim around their tank. Kevin was careful not to remove them from the tank since the scare of losing them. His Mother said, "No Kevin. I'm sorry, but the family is visiting your grandma this Labor Day weekend". Kevin asked if he could bring Chester and Julie to grandma's. His mother said "No–the turtles will stay behind this weekend". So, Kevin began to pack for the weekend away from home.

Kevin woke up extra early the next morning to clean the turtle tank and leave enough food since he would be leaving his turtles behind for the weekend. He placed the turtles in a cereal bowl on his window sill while he cleaned the tank and prepared enough food to last Saturday, Sunday, and Monday. The family left for a 2-hour road trip to visit his grandma. But Kevin forgot to place the turtles back into their turtle tank before leaving!

It was forecasted to be a very hot weekend. Kevin's mother turned off the air conditioner before the family left. Chester and Julie were in the cereal bowl with no cool air, water, or food. Chester was worried about Julie because he knew he was bigger and stronger than her. It was very warm in the house. The sun rays were shining on the cereal bowl causing it to get hotter as time passed. Julie became weak, tired, and sunburned. Her shell did not protect her from the heat. Chester knew it would be dark soon and it would finally cool off again. Julie stopped moving and seemed to be sleeping inside her shell. Chester kept a watchful eye on her and nudged Julie a few times to wake her up. But Julie never woke up again. Chester feared he would also not wake up if he fell asleep.

In this book you will learn how to take care of your pet turtle, how to feed your turtle, how to create a safe onment for your turtle and more.

COMPLETE GUIDE TO
Caring for Your
PET TURTLE

Kevin and his family returned home early Monday morning. Kevin rushed inside his room to greet Chester and Julie. He saw the Goldfish bowl was empty and realized that he left them in the cereal bowl accidently. Kevin was shocked at the sight of the poor turtles in the hot dry cereal bowl on the windowsill. He carefully lifted Chester and Julie from the bowl and placed them back in the Goldfish bowl. Chester was very thirsty and hungry. He was a strong swimmer and rushed to the food and water. But Julie never came back out of her shell. Julie died from the heat exhaustion and dehydration. Kevin and Chester wept for Julie. The family buried Julie in the backyard. Kevin's mother helped soothe the pain of losing Julie by assuring Kevin that Julie was in turtle heaven. Kevin's mother bought him a book teaching him how to care for pet turtles. She read the book to Kevin before bed each night. Kevin learned how to take care of Chester and how to keep him safe going forward.

Chester missed his sister Julie very much, but he knew that turtle heaven was a nice place and Julie was playing and having fun in a glass bowl sitting on a cloud with clean rainwater. Kevin never forgot his mistake and every day he made sure Chester was out of harm's way. Kevin saved his allowance to buy a second container for Chester to stay in while his bowl was being cleaned. Kevin knew Chester loved him because every time Kevin was near the tank, Chester raised his head high to greet Kevin. Kevin learned to lift him from the tank holding the middle of his shell and to softly rub his chin and cheeks. Chester learned to trust Kevin and he would never withdraw to his shell when Kevin was nearby. Chester was happy when he sat on Kevin's lap and he never crawl off. Chester and Kevin had a very strong bond. Chester's bowl was large, and he swam freely from side to side underwater. Chester would enjoy dinner and afterward bask in the sunlight on his rocks and then fall fast asleep.

Kevin's mother announced that the family needed to sell their house, move to the city, and live in an apartment. Kevin was very worried that he would not be allowed to keep his beloved Chester in the apartment since many landlords do not allow pets. His mother said, "Chester is family and will move to the city with us". They all moved to the city in a small 2-bedroom apartment with an outdoor sunroom. Kevin bought Chester a new fish tank and placed it in the sunroom. Chester's Fish Tank was placed in the sunroom, it was screen covered and had plenty of sunlight with a beautiful view of the mountains. The climate was very mild all year round and the sunroom was just outside Kevin's bedroom and a perfect place for Chester to live. Chester did not mind that the washer and dryer was placed in the sunroom because he got to have visits from all the family members whenever they did their laundry.

Kevin started a new school, quickly made new friends, and continued to take great care of Chester. Chester enjoyed his new room, and he spent most days swimming, eating, napping, and playing with his rock toys. Chester was getting bored waiting for Kevin to arrive home from school every day. So, Chester thought about climbing out of the Fish Tank and exploring the rest of the new apartment. The Fish Tank was deep, but he noticed the seaweed grew all the way to the top of the tank. Chester tried to climb up the branches and fell back into the water. Chester was determined to venture out, so he tried again and again. He fell each time and wondered if the branches of the seaweed could not hold his weight. Chester grew weary of continuously climbing the seaweed and falling off and decided to call it a night.

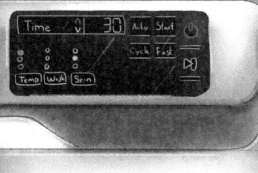

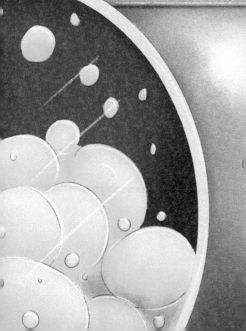
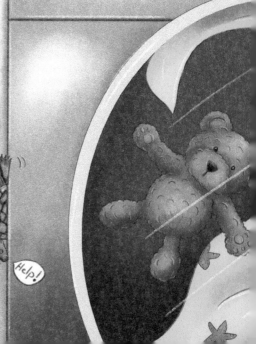

Chester woke up the next morning still determined to climb to the top of the seaweed and jump out of the Fish Tank onto the ledge so that he could explore his new surroundings. He finally made it to the top of the tank! Chester was very excited about his new adventure! He leaped from the tank, missed the ledge, and fell in the tiny space between the washer and dryer. Chester hissed and cried, but no one heard him. He could not move because he was lodged between the machines so tight. Chester was very scared and unsure if Kevin would ever find him.

Kevin was running late and had to skip his morning visit with Chester. So he was anxious to get through the school today and come home to see his buddy Chester and take a walk with him. Finally, the school day ended, and Kevin hurried home to see Chester. He raced all the way home as fast as his legs could run. Kevin opened the door to the porch overjoyed to spend time with Chester. But... the tank was empty! Kevin thought that Chester must be hiding from him under the seashells. Kevin looked closely into the Fish Tank but there was no turtle anywhere in sight.

Kevin dashed into the house calling, "Mom, mom, where are you"?! Kevin's mom knew that something was wrong. Kevin spoke and sobbed until his mom finally understood that Chester was missing. They searched every inch of the porch, but Chester was not found. They moved all the furniture from the porch and looked everywhere and still- no Chester. They were afraid that a predator had gotten Chester. Chester could not be seen by anyone. Chester was very scared and worried that he would never be found. With all the moving of the furniture and with Kevin's screaming, no one could hear Chester's hissing and cries. Kevin's mom asked him to calm down and to stop crying. She gently picked him up and sat him on the dryer. Kevin put his head down, ashamed about crying a river of tears. Suddenly, he heard a noise sounding like Chester hissing! Kevin looked down and saw Chester's hind legs wiggling. He rescued Chester from the tight space gently and looked for any signs of damage to his shell. Chester lifted his head and gave Kevin a smile of relief. The family was so thankful that Chester was alive and okay!

Kevin had a dentist appointment the next day. He decided to remove the seaweed from Chester's tank to make sure that he did not try to climb out again. During the dental visit, Dr. Tortoise, the dentist noticed that Kevin was troubled, and he asked why. Kevin told Dr. Tortoise he had a pet turtle, but he was not a very good owner with all that happened to Chester and Julie. Kevin learned from his mom that one must be older to take on the responsibility of caring for a living being. His dentist offered to adopt Chester since he owned 3 pet turtles and had lot of experience. Kevin agreed that it would be best for Chester to be with Dr. Tortoise. Later that day, Kevin said his tearful goodbyes to Chester and the turtle moved in with Dr. Tortoise to join his 3 other turtles.

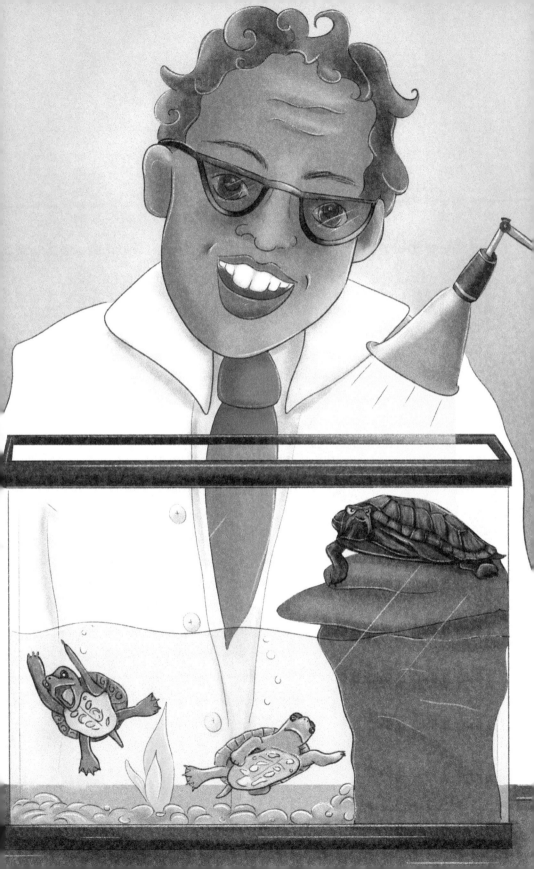

The other turtles did not warm up to Chester. They were larger and did not want to share their tank with a small turtle. The largest of the three turtles splashed water on Chester. The other two would not allow Chester to eat or rest on the rocks. They were mean turtles and did not want to share their home with Chester. In the middle of the night, Dr. Tortoise heard excessive splashing and action in the turtle tank. He decided to investigate what all the disturbance was about. The two medium size turtles were splashing, jumping and hitting the rocks against the tank. Dr. Tortoise noticed Chester was in the mouth of the larger turtle and he was chewing on Chester's shell. Dr. Tortoise yanked Chester out his mouth just in time to save Chester's life. Chester and Dr. Tortoise took a big sigh of relief!

Dr. Tortoise removed Chester from the tank with the other 3 turtles and he slept on a pillow that night. The very next day, a brand-new turtle tank arrived for Chester! The tank came with a heater to keep the water warm. It was big and could hold 40 gallons of water. It also came with live underwater plants, seashells of all different sizes and colors, rocks, sand, and a small terrain to eliminate climbing out of the tank. Chester smiled at Dr. Tortoise and said to himself, "This is a happy home"! The other turtles adapted to Chester's new tank placed next to theirs and life at Dr. Tortoise home went back to normal. Chester hoped for a visit from his best friend Kevin soon because he missed him terribly.

The next day, Chester was lying on the rocks facing the other turtle tank and the larger turtle sneered through the glass at Chester. He also bumped the tank very forcefully trying to break Chester's tank glass. Chester feared the large turtle since he tried to devour him a few days earlier. Chester remembered how scary it was be in the mouth of that big turtle.

Chester decided to make a kind gesture toward him. He figured it always helped to be kind to a mean-spirited friend or foe. Chester swam upside down, side to side, and as fast as he could and flipped over a few times to show his good and kind nature trying to soften the big turtle. Chester also tossed food into the other turtles' tank in case they were hungry. The other two turtles watched Chester do tricks and seemed amused by Chester's expression of fun! Chester worried because the larger turtle was not swayed. He continued to bump the tank glass and splash water angrily. Chester really missed the love, affection and protection Kevin gave him.

Dr. Tortoise noticed Chester hiding behind the rocks in his tank all day as if he did not want the other turtles to see him. Dr. Tortoise was unaware of why Chester was in hiding. He thought a trip to the beach and a long walk with Chester would make him feel better. Dr. Tortoise thought it would be a nice outing to pick up Kevin and for all three of them to spend the day having a picnic on the

Santa Monica Beach. Dr. Tortoise called Kevin's mom and decided to pick up Kevin early the next morning. Dr. Tortoise went over to Chester's tank excited and happy to tell Chester of the plans to spend the day at the beach with his friend Kevin. Chester marveled at the idea of seeing Kevin tomorrow!

Dr. Tortoise, Kevin, and Chester left at 9:00AM and headed to the Santa Monica Beach. It was a windy cool morning, but it would warm up in an hour or less. They arrived at 11:30AM to find calm waters, small blue glowing waves, clean white sand, and a warm sunny day. It was a perfect day for a picnic, and everyone was excited to lie on the beach towels and have a bite to eat. Dr. Tortoise and Kevin ate shrimp sandwiches, drank water, and Chester munched on apples. Chester was overjoyed, Kevin was tickled, and Dr. Tortoise was very pleased. They watched the waves build into a large swell as the wind picked up again. Kevin and Chester were busy building sandcastles that started to blow away.

The tide was rushing in, the waves were crashing ashore, and the new waves were rising to surfing levels! Dr. Tortoise suggested that they take a walk on the beach since the weather was changing, they would need to leave soon. Dr. Tortoise and Kevin walked ahead of Chester since his legs were shorter and turtles walk more slowly. Chester was suddenly swept away by one the waves and found himself in another dangerous predicament! Dr. Tortoise and Kevin looked around and did not see Chester anywhere. They began a frantic search for him, Dr. Tortoise jumped into the ocean and swam for hours searching for Chester. Kevin scanned the beach tirelessly hoping and praying Chester would wash ashore and come back to them.

Chester swam as fast as his tiny legs could in the strong ripples and the enormous swells of waves. They carried the small turtle fast and furiously. Chester noticed a whale nearby. He thought he may survive the waves and density of the ocean if he hopped on the fin of Mr. Whale. He figured

the whale may not even notice him because of his small size. And the whale was so massive in size and a very strong swimmer and was feared amongst other sea enemies. Everyone thinks sharks are the dominant terror of the waters, but Chester knew he would be safe and have a fun ride on the blue whale since they roam the world's oceans. Whales are warm blooded mammals and love to care for their families.

Blue Whales also eat Chester's favorite food: plankton and they also breathe air when they are above the ocean water. This would be a perfect ride to shore. Chester was fully aware that whales travel to the Sea of Cortez in February to either mate or have babies. Chester hoped this blue whale would take him to Mexico and that there was a small chance that he would meet his beloved human family there on vacation. Kevin's mom planned to take the family on vacation to watch whales in Cabo San Lucas in February. Chester latched on to the friendly whale and headed for Mexico feeling excited for the adventure but also missing his best friend Kevin dearly hoping they would meet again.

Kevin and Dr. Tortoise never found Chester. Kevin knew Chester knew how to survive life threating situations that he found himself in many times. Kevin and Dr. Tortoise went home full of hope that they would see Chester again someday.

The End.